MAKING FRIENDS WITH MY EMOTIONS

IT'S OK TO BE SURPRISED

THERESA EMMINIZER

PowerKiDS press

Published in 2025 by The Rosen Publishing Group, Inc.
2544 Clinton Street, Buffalo, NY 14224

First Edition

Editor: Theresa Emminizer
Book Design: Michael Flynn

Photo Credits: Cover, p. 1 AJP/Shutterstock.com; (series background) Sergei Mishchenko/Shutterstock.com; p. 5 Prostock-studio/Shutterstock.com; p. 7 Pressmaster/Shutterstock.com; p. 9 Jacob Lund/Shutterstock.com; p. 11 Bricolage/Shutterstock.com; p. 13 Ixepop/Shutterstock.com; p. 15 UfaBizPhoto/Shutterstock.com; p. 17 takayuki/Shutterstock.com; p. 19 Yuliia Lisiana/Shutterstock.com; p. 21 Yuliia Lisiana/Shutterstock.com.

Library of Congress Cataloging-in-Publication Data

Names: Emminizer, Theresa, author.
Title: It's ok to be surprised / Theresa Emminizer.
Description: [Buffalo] : PowerKids Press, [2025] | Series: Making friends with my emotions | Includes bibliographical references and index. |
Audience: Grades K-1
Identifiers: LCCN 2023054206 (print) | LCCN 2023054207 (ebook) | ISBN 9781499445084 (library binding) | ISBN 9781499445077 (paperback) | ISBN 9781499445091 (ebook)
Subjects: LCSH: Surprise in children–Juvenile literature. |
Surprise–Juvenile literature.
Classification: LCC BF723.S87 E46 2025 (print) | LCC BF723.S87 (ebook) |
DDC 155.4/136–dc23/eng/20231218
LC record available at https://lccn.loc.gov/2023054206
LC ebook record available at https://lccn.loc.gov/2023054207

Manufactured in the United States of America

CPSIA Compliance Information: Batch #CSPK25. For Further Information contact Rosen Publishing at 1-800-237-9932.

CONTENTS

Feeling Surprised

Surprise! Surprise is what you feel when something happens that you didn't expect! When you're surprised you might feel **tingly**, like there are butterflies in your stomach. You might gasp, or take a big gulp of air. Your eyes might open wide. Your heart might pound.

Happy Surprises

There are lots of happy surprises. They can be small, like getting a gift you weren't expecting. Or big, like coming home to a surprise birthday party. These kinds of surprises can be **exciting**. They make life fun and interesting and put a smile on your face.

Hooray!

Alice missed her dad. He had been away for a long time. Alice didn't expect him home for weeks. Suddenly, Alice heard a voice outside. It was her dad! He came home early to surprise Alice! Alice jumped in her dad's arms.

Unhappy Surprises

Although lots of surprises are happy, some of them don't feel good. You might feel surprised when things don't turn out the way you hoped they would. Maybe you planned to go to the beach, but there's a storm outside. That kind of surprise can be hard.

A Big Surprise

Eli was feeling confused. His mom just told him that he was going to be a big brother. Eli was sort of happy. But he felt sad too. This was a big surprise. Eli thought it'd just be him and his mom always.

Mixed Feelings

When something surprising happens, it can bring up lots of different feelings. Sometimes we feel both good and bad about the surprise. That's called having mixed feelings and it's OK! Unexpected changes can be hard. But there are many ways to **cope**.

Share Your Feelings

Surprises might make you feel out of control. Even happy surprises! Feeling out of control can be a little bit scary. Talking to an adult you trust can help. A safe adult will never make you feel bad. They'll listen and try to help!

Let It Out!

Even happy surprises can feel **overwhelming**. That's okay! If you feel tears come into your eyes, let them fall. Crying can help release, or let out, your feelings. We cry for all sorts of different reasons, happy or sad. There's nothing wrong with that.

Have Confidence

Life is full of surprises! Some are happy, some are not. It helps to know you aren't alone. Everybody feels surprised sometimes! And feelings don't last forever. Trust yourself. Know that no matter what comes your way, you can cope. Remember, it's OK to be surprised!

GLOSSARY

cope: Dealing with or working through your feelings.

exciting: Something that makes you feel lively and happy.

overwhelming: Very strong or overpowering.

tingly: A prickly feeling.

FOR MORE INFORMATION

BOOKS

McAneney, Caitie. *I Breathe to Cope.* New York, NY: PowerKids Press, 2023.

McAneney, Caitie. *I Talk to Cope.* New York, NY: PowerKids Press, 2023.

WEBSITES

British Council
learnenglishkids.britishcouncil.org/songs/feelings-are-feelings
Listen to songs and play games about feelings.

Kids Health
kidshealth.org/en/kids/talk-feelings.html
Learn how to name and talk about your feelings.

Publisher's note to educators and parents: Our editors have carefully reviewed these websites to ensure that they are suitable for students. Many websites change frequently, however, and we cannot guarantee that a site's future contents will continue to meet our high standards of quality and educational value. Be advised that students should be closely supervised whenever they access the internet.

INDEX